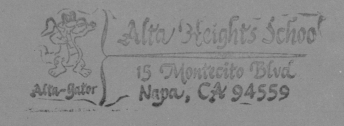

Bag in the Wind ❧

Bag in the Wind

TED KOOSER   ILLUSTRATED BY BARRY ROOT

CANDLEWICK PRESS

One cold, windy morning early in spring, a bulldozer was pushing a big pile of garbage around a landfill when it uncovered an empty plastic bag. The woman driving the bulldozer didn't notice the bag and drove on. It was a bag for carrying groceries, just the color of the skin of a yellow onion, and it had two holes for handles. It was a perfectly good bag, but someone had thrown it away.

All through the day, the wind tugged at the bag and shifted it
around, and then there came a big gust, and the bag filled with air
and began to somersault across the landfill, leaping over empty cans
and bottles and plastic drink cups and fast-food hamburger boxes.

It rolled and flapped all the way to a chain-link fence at one side of the landfill, where it got pressed up against the wire with a lot of other trash—newspapers, candy wrappers, and Styrofoam cups. As the night came on the wind died down, and the bag slipped along the fence and lay all night next to the gate.

There was a shack by the gate, and in the morning a man in a cap with earflaps came to sit in the window with a clipboard. The garbage trucks came and went, roaring and groaning under their loads. When they arrived at the gate, the drivers pulled the trucks up over a big scale that had been set into the road. When the man in the shack had written down the weight, he waved them on, and they rolled ahead into the landfill. After they had dumped their loads, they came back across the scale and were weighed again, and the difference in the two weights was the number of pounds of garbage they had brought to the landfill. The more pounds they brought, the more money the drivers had to pay the man in the window. This went on until the sun was low in the west. Then the man locked the gate for the night and drove away.

Soon it got dark, and the stars came out, and clouds like enormous black leaf bags raced across the moon. A puff of cold wind got in under the grocery bag and lifted it high in the air.

It went up and over the fence and was blown along a roadside ditch with water trickling along it. The bag bounded along over dirty snowdrifts that still lay in the shadows of the ditch banks.

There were lots of young trees along the ditch, their twigs covered with hard little buds that would soon open, and the bag got caught on a branch and hung there the rest of the night, flapping and slapping in the wind.

In the morning, it was a little warmer but still very windy. A red-winged blackbird perched a few feet away, bobbing in the top of a little willow tree, and it whistled angrily at the bag because the bird thought it was an owl or raccoon that had invaded its territory. After a while, it began to fly at the bag again and again, flapping its wings as if to frighten it away and pecking it with its sharp beak. Finally, the bird got hold of the bag with its beak and gave it a sharp tug, and the bag pulled free and blew away.

The bag rolled for a long way along the side of a country road and then got caught on a barbed-wire fence at the edge of a muddy field. After a while, a girl came walking along, all bundled up against the cold. Her coat pockets were full of crushed aluminum cans.

"Good!" she said. "There's a bag I can use for these cans!" She unhooked the bag from the fence and emptied her pockets into it. Then she went on down the road, whistling a little tune, carrying the bag full of cans, and picking up more cans as she found them.

A couple of miles farther down the road, there was a funny little gas station. It had a flagpole with the American flag flapping in the wind. There were two gas pumps in front and an old washing machine with a wringer for wringing out rags around the side. There were signs nailed all over the walls reading TIRES and AIR and GREASE JOBS and CANDY and CLEAN RESTROOMS and FRESH-GROWN VEGETABLES. It didn't look as if anybody was there, but as the girl came nearer, a woman in a long coat and a headscarf came out the door.

"Got some cans to cash in, I see!" the woman said with a smile.

"Yes, that's right," said the girl, holding the bag.

The old woman took the bag from the girl and led her into the building, where she set the bag on a scale. "I can give you eighteen cents a pound today, Margaret!" she said. "And you've got two pounds here. That makes thirty-six cents." She pulled out a long leather purse with snaps on the top and shook out some coins and put them in Margaret's outstretched hand. There were three dimes, a nickel, and a penny.

"Thank you," the girl said.

"What are you going to do with the money?" asked the old woman.

"I'm saving up for something special," said Margaret.

"Well, you just keep picking up those cans," said the woman. "The road sure looks a lot nicer, all picked up like that."

When the girl had gone, the old woman put the cans in a barrel, then she wedged the grocery bag under the door to stop some of the wind from getting in.

Next she sat down on a chair beside the window so she could see if someone pulled off the road for gas.

After a while, a man in a pickup pulled in to fill up with gas. The back of his truck was full of plastic bags stuffed with leaves. When the old woman went out the door to pump the gas, she didn't notice that the grocery bag came loose from under the door and blew a few feet along the front of the building.

"Where are you going with all those leaves?" the old woman asked.

"I'm going to dump them at the landfill," the man answered, getting out of the truck. He rubbed his hands together to warm them. All you could see of his face was his red nose sticking out of his hood.

"You'll have to pay the man at the gate, you know," the old woman said. "He charges five dollars for a pickup load. Why don't you just set the bags along the north side of the station here? You'll see some other ones there. They keep the drafts out till spring, and then I use the leaves for mulch and compost for my garden."

"Why, sure! I'm glad to save the money!" The man smiled, and he began to carry the bags around the building.

Just then, a gust of wind came down the road, carrying chewing gum wrappers and pieces of cornstalk, and it snatched up the grocery bag and carried it away. There was nothing to catch the bag this time, and it blew and rolled and flapped along for several miles. Sometimes the wind died down and the bag would lie still for a minute, but then a car or truck would whistle past and the wind would pick up the bag and send it flapping on.

It was beginning to get dark again, and the wind was sharp and cold. A tall man with long hair and a beard came limping along the side of the road, using a metal crutch. The bag came rolling along the shoulder toward him, and he caught it with the tip of his crutch. He leaned down and picked it up and wadded it into his pocket with a lot of other things: a box of matches, a little book with a leather cover, and a few lemon-flavored cough drops covered with lint. Then he went down the road.

After a while, the man came to a stream that went through a big concrete culvert under the road, and he climbed down the bank. The culvert had a wall around the opening, and he sat down with his back up against the wall, out of the wind. He rubbed the cold out of his big red hands and took a bag of corn chips out of his backpack and ate a few. Then he got up and collected twigs and sticks and built a campfire. The smoke from the fire made him cough, and he pulled the grocery bag out of his coat pocket while he dug around for a cough drop.

He left the bag on the ground, and it slowly came unwadded. Soon a breeze began to nudge it away from the man's side. The man was sleepy, and he got a big black leaf bag out of his pack and pulled it over his feet and lay down with his knees pulled up against his chest. Inch by inch the grocery bag rolled toward the ribbon of water flowing into the culvert, and soon the water had carried it away.

There was just enough air in the bag to keep it floating, and the bag rode along on the surface of the stream through the dark culvert and out into the night on the other side of the road. Above it, stars twinkled, cold and distant. The moon was rising. Wind hurried the bag downstream on the shiny black water, and soon the stream widened, fed by trickles from ditches and foamy water from big pipes that came out of the banks.

All night the bag floated in this wide river, which was lined by silent warehouses, their tall windows reflecting the dawn. Boats and barges were anchored in the river or tied up to docks—fishing boats and tugboats and barges heaped with trash. Gulls flew in circles, calling to one another, and then they folded their wings and landed to pick through the garbage.

The bag blew across the surface of the river and up alongside a dock. A woman was camped there and was just rolling up her sleeping bag to put it away in her grocery cart. She saw the bag at the edge of the water and picked it up and shook the water from it. Then she stuffed it in the front of her outside coat.

The woman pushed the cart down the street a few blocks to a corner where a woman was serving the people on the street doughnuts and coffee from the back of a station wagon.

"Good morning," the woman said. "Would you like some doughnuts and coffee?"

The woman nodded and snatched a doughnut from a box, and as she did, the grocery bag fell out of her coat. She didn't notice it.

When a gust of wind blew the grocery bag out from under the woman's feet, a man in a cowboy hat ran after it and caught it and stuffed it inside his leather jacket.

The man had a three-wheeled bicycle with a big basket on the back piled high with plastic bags. He put the grocery bag in with the others.

The man got on his bike and pedaled a couple of blocks down the street to a secondhand store. A thin woman in a cardigan sweater was sweeping the sidewalk in front of the store. Her hair was curled up in plastic rollers.

"I've got some bags for you," the man said.

"I can see that," she answered. "Looks like quite a few." She leaned on her broom.

"More than I could ever count," the man said. "Can you give me two dollars for them?"

The woman squinched up her face. "No, but maybe a dollar, though. I just bought a big pile from you last week, and I still have some left."

The man took the dollar, and the woman carried the bags into the store.

Just then a girl walked in. It was Margaret.

"Do you have any baseball gloves?" she asked the woman.

"Right over there," the woman answered, pointing to a crate full of baseball gloves and catcher's masks and balls and bats.

Margaret looked through the crate and found just exactly the glove she'd been saving her money to buy. She tried it on, and it fit perfectly. "How much is this one?" she asked.

"Only five dollars," said the woman.

"I'll take it!" said Margaret. "And that leaves me an extra dollar. Can I buy a baseball with a dollar?"

The woman thought for a moment. "Sure, I guess so," she said.

Margaret gave the woman the money, and the woman rang up the sale. Then she said, "Let's put them in a bag for you." She went to the pile of bags the man in the cowboy hat had sold her and picked out a bag and put the glove and ball in it.

It was the very same grocery bag that Margaret had used to collect cans in, but Margaret didn't recognize it because it looked just like every other grocery bag in the world—the color of the skin of a yellow onion, with two holes for handles.

A NOTE ABOUT RECYCLING PLASTIC BAGS ❧

Americans use 100 billion plastic shopping bags per year, which means that the average American—both kids and adults—uses between 350 and 500 bags per year. Most plastic grocery bags get used only once and are then thrown away. In a garbage dump, it might take anywhere from fifteen to a thousand years for a plastic bag to decompose because plastic photodegrades, which means it breaks down when exposed to sunlight. Because landfills pile garbage very deep, a lot of plastic waste doesn't get exposed to light and therefore takes a very long time to break down. Also, many bags fly away from landfills and trash cans, and those bags can be very dangerous for animals who mistake them for food or get tangled in them. A million birds and 100,000 sea turtles and other animals die every year due to ingesting plastic bags or getting them caught around their necks, wings, or legs.

Be sure to reuse any plastic bags you have in your home. Take them with you when you go shopping so you don't have to use new plastic bags. They can also be used as trash-can liners, lunch bags, and to line your cat's litter box or to clean up after the dog. Check to see if your local library, animal shelter, food pantry, or secondhand store might collect bags for reuse.

Plastic bags can also be recycled, but they can't always be collected with curbside recycling programs. Do some research around your neighborhood—many grocery stores take them back, for example.

Plastic bags should definitely be reused and recycled, but the best thing to do is to stop using plastic bags altogether. If you—just you!—use reusable cloth bags instead of plastic bags, you could save over 22,000 plastic bags all by yourself in your lifetime!

Here are some useful resources:

www.plasticbagrecycling.org

www.onebagatatime.com

To the memory of Dace Burdic, recycler and beloved friend

T. K.

For Janna

B. R.

Text copyright © 2010 by Ted Kooser
Illustrations copyright © 2010 by Barry Root

First edition 2010

Library of Congress Cataloging-in-Publication Data

Kooser, Ted.
Bag in the wind / Ted Kooser ; illustrated by Barry Root. —1st U.S. ed.
p. cm.
Summary: One cold, spring morning, an ordinary grocery bag begins blowing around
a landfill, then as it travels down a road, through a stream, and into a town, it is used
in various ways by different people, many of whom do not even notice it.
ISBN 978-0-7636-3001-0
[1. Bags—Fiction. 2. Recycling (Waste)—Fiction. 3. Sanitary landfills—Fiction.]
I. Root, Barry, ill. II. Title.
PZ7.K885775Bag 2010
(E)—dc22   2009022088

09 10 11 12 13 14 CCP 10 9 8 7 6 5 4 3 2 1

Printed in Shenzhen, Guangdong, China

This book was typeset in Colwell.
The illustrations were done in watercolor and gouache.

✪ This paper contains 100% recycled post-consumer waste.

Candlewick Press
99 Dover Street
Somerville, Massachusetts 02144

visit us at www.candlewick.com